Girls

Volume 1

Jo Vraca

DEDICATION

Where to begin? Only one place, really: Jeff, for believing that I can write, for continuing to read what I write even if it's not his bag. He's a patient man who doesn't complain when I ask for time away from the world— and that means: no work, take-away dinners, no fun, just writing, and my own (very noisy) headspace that comes out at the most inappropriate moments. Thanks to my friends for playing board games in one room while I write in another. Thanks to Arran for editing the finished words. Thanks to Melbourne's Western suburbs for giving me ample sights to write about.

Stories

On the Seventh Day

Monday

He moves around a lot. I just lie there sucking on the fig, pink and white pulp crushed against my sticky lips.

His body makes a neat table, perfect angles to rest my cup upon, if I was drinking tea, or even the figs and apples, which are on the window ledge right in front of his face. I've placed them in a row, purple, green, purple, green, purple, green, purple. By Sunday, the ants will have begun to investigate the syrupy aroma.

He looks down at me curiously; is it as good for you…

Of course, you're the best.

His face sparkles like a plum after heavy rain. A damp strand of hair is playing with his eyelashes and I want to pull him close, lay his face against my cheek. Instead I pull the meagre hair on his chest.

"I wish you wouldn't do that," he says. He moves his hips gently against mine.

"Sorry." I move my hand away slowly, brushing his nipples.

"No, not that. That."

"What?"

"That. Eat while we fuck. You know I hate that slurping."

Papa used to tell me to chew more delicately, and to close my mouth. But I would gasp for air between bites.

"I'm hungry."

My eyes sting with sweat. I wriggle out from beneath him and lie there, resting on my elbows and looking out of the window above the bed head while he gets dressed behind me.

Across the courtyard that separates the east and west wings of the apartment building, the redheaded dancer finally appears on the cramped balcony. She stretches her legs and arms, her feet en pointe, aiming her hands desperately to the balcony above as though trying to tear her body in two.

She pirouettes and her skirt flips over her belly, revealing a shock of waist-high white briefs.

Tuesday

"'You never take me anywhere, always stuck in this house like I'm some godforsaken vestal virgin, f'god'ssake.'"

He's a goddamn bore when he starts talking like this, but he pays well so I'm not about to start.

"That's exactly what she said to me. Can you believe that? I give her so many goddamn diamonds that she might want to use some to plug up that fat mouth. Death by diamonds." He snorts at the gag.

"Tell me you would shut up if you got diamonds. And not just any diamonds—square ones, rectangular ones, round ones with so many facets that you can see ever blackhead, goddamn it. I even gave the bitch a pink one. No cubic zirconia from me, honey. Bitch walks around half her life in those slippers that have a heel like a prostitute's—no offence— and that mangy dog tucked under her arm—even when she eats!—and then she complains to me that I'm never home. Vestal virgin? I wish."

In all actuality, I suspect that Charlie Conti is gay and that he has no wife. In fact, I'm certain of it. But I'm not about to stop him from going on and on. He doesn't like me to talk much, unless he asks a direct question, like, "Octavia what time is it?" or "Octavia did you have a bath this morning?" or "Octavia, do you love me?"

I have nothing to add to his outbursts. Often, though, I just tune him out.

The dancer across the courtyard is lying on the washed-out carpet just inside her balcony. She's holding a grey kitten against her face, rubbing it against her skin like it's a washcloth.

She tickles its nose with hers and the kitten bats her lips playfully.

"—alone?"

My nose is cold and slightly moist, like a dog's. The weather's turning, as is the fruit on the peppercorn tree that darkens the courtyard, from pink to brown to black.

"Did you catch that?" Charlie says through sad lips.

"What?" I turn back to him and twirl the apple stem—A, B, C... —until it twists off. Always a J.

"I'm leaving," Charlie says in that way he has when he's trying to make me feel guilty for ignoring him or something.

"Don't go." I mean it. I'm not ready to be alone yet.

I climb across the bed and wrap my arms around his hips, my head in his warm thighs.

"Why stay?" He falls back on the bed.

"Because I like you to."

I rub his earlobes. He likes that.

"But you're never here. Always so far—"

I turn his face towards me and his eyes are glistening.

"No, no, I'm here, I swear. I'm listening now. I mean, I was listening before but I just missed some of it."

He goes back to what he was doing and I turn back to the window. She's whispering into the cat's ear. Warm, soft, smelling of the musk lollies that she keeps in the glass jar next to the sofa.

Wednesday

Willie drives an electric-blue Chevy pickup truck with red flames that lick the side panels, black wall-to-wall carpet interior and a crucifix hanging from his rear-view mirror.

He hangs out at the local high schools and looks at the girls even though he's just served a stint for fucking a girl who had "tits that were too big and an ass too curvy to be only fifteen".

He has a thing for Viagra too.

"I am willing to see my magnificence."

He turns back from the bedside table and I stop poring over the fruit; the figs have already started to sag.

"What?"

"I am willing to see my magnificence."

"Okay."

I turn back. I'm distracted by the poor-quality fruit. I pick up the fig from the stem and it sticks to the window ledge momentarily.

Her apartment is smaller than mine. It's a bedsit too but the sofa is closer to the bed.

She's in the kitchen tossing the contents of a frying pan into the air like they do in infomercials. Her sinewy arms tense with the effort.

Willie slaps my ass and laughs, and I'm back in the room for a moment.

"Yes, yes, I see it too," I say.

"No, that's what it says on this card. Where'd you get this shit from?"

I turn to face him. He's holding a square green card from the deck that's under the lamp on the bedside table. My Dream Cards. How embarrassing, I forgot to put them back last night.

"Oh it's nothing, it's just something—"

A scream echoes across the way.

She's shaking her hands nervously and the frying pan's on the floor, its contents splattered everywhere.

Hold it under cold running water. I wish I could leap across the ten yards that divide us and blow cool air on the wound.

"What are you looking at? Say, who's tha—"

I turn back to him quickly and settle him with my hand. He rests his head back onto the pillow.

The dancer is sitting on the sagging sofa now, on top of the throw that's covered in large pastel peonies. She's just staring at her hand.

I look at my free hand and hold it to my cheek.

Alone. Forgotten.

Do the dancer's eyes ever wander beyond the confines of her tired walls? Does she ever watch me?

Thursday

"Are the waters calm there?"

"Why aren't you here?" I'm feeling vague today.

The dancer is on the sofa, holding a feather above the kitten's head, flicking it over its nose and paws. Her hand is bandaged with gauze the colour of flamingos.

"Are the waters calm there?"

"What waters?"

"The waters!"

"There's no water here. I'm inland. You said you'd be back in time."

"What a shame."

"I rely on it."

She moves like a ballerina. She doesn't walk through her apartment. She does a plié to remove a carton of milk from the refrigerator, a pirouette to add a pinch of salt to a pot.

"Can I come next week instead?" He's anxious now.

"I'll have to check my schedule."

I don't have the energy for this today. He's a whiny dog, begging for scraps. A spoilt child with no toys.

"I know you must be so busy but I just wish the waters were calm so I could just dip my toes for a while."

But I told you there is no water here, I want to scream into the receiver. But I close my eyes and count instead.

"Tell me what you're wearing," he sighs.

No energy for this. I'm off the clock right now.

"I'm sorry, I can't make much time for a phone call at the moment."

She bends forward and wraps her long arms around her calves, folding at the middle like a rag doll. The skin on her back is like parchment stretched over her ribs. She remains in this position, her body rising and falling with each breath, shaking with every sigh.

I don't want to, but I take a bite from the apple and concentrate on the voice on the other end of the line.

Friday

Daniel had spent three months in Japan wandering through the S & M clubs where they eat sushi off naked bodies. Consequently, he has developed a penchant for unblemished, milky flesh and carefully embroidered silks that he likes to drape across my thighs.

I fall asleep for a few moments, my head resting on the open book. I wake to something cool and pasty on my back. Something dribbles down my waist but I try to ignore it. I also try to ignore the slurping but I like the sensation of his warm tongue against my skin.

He inhales deeply.

"Those Japanese are too clever for their own good."

"I heard once that in America they have chocolate with chillies in it," I mumble through the pages of the book.

"Oh, this is much better." He slaps my thigh enthusiastically.

I am rather fond of his enthusiasm.

There is a sound from across the courtyard. I look up and she is pressed against her front door. Someone is pounding on it.

"Faustina!" says a man's voice from the other side of the door. The voice, all menace and low notes, collides with the loud and tinny gypsy music that echoes through the peppercorn tree.

Faustina.

How about that…

She clasps the opening of her kimono and wraps the belt tightly around her wrist, one time around, two times, three. She hurtles herself wildly towards the tape player and turns the volume up until I can't hear the voice behind the door.

Faustina resumes her protective post against the rattling door. She places her hands over her ears and the robe falls open, revealing a Bermuda patch of flat, dark hairs and a scar from her naval to the top of her ribs zipping her closed neatly.

Daniel groans loudly and I blink my attention back to the room.

Saturday

He just wants my company today. Father Alfonzo Agosti scatters the pieces of the Vatican, all five hundred of them, onto the flattened sheet with the yellowing embroidery stitches.

The first time I saw her, Faustina, was the day that Father Alfonzo Agosti first came calling. She was hanging a white slip over a cord that was tied across her balcony.

"Are you a virgin?" he asked when I greeted him at the door.

I was thrown. You see, it isn't a question I get asked much. Not at all, actually. So I didn't manage to respond quickly enough. The eyes behind the rimless hexagonal glasses were disapproving. No, they were disappointed.

"Of course, Father," I blurted.

Things have gone swimmingly ever since.

He wears a civilian suit when he comes. A gold cross rests under his shirt against his skin. Before his first appointment, I imagined he would be like the Jesuit priest from *The Exorcist*—the one played by Jason Miller. I imagined he would be young and athletic. Instead, Father Alfonzo Agosti is middle aged and short. But he does have a spectacular head of hair.

To my delight, Father Alfonzo Agosti does not waste his time with meaningless chitchat. His visits are solemn like confession. I arch my spine to meet his smooth fingers, which have never done an honest day's work.

He strokes me now, under my arms, and offers me an apple. The sun has bleached it slightly on one side. I take a bite and spit it into the priest's waiting hands. He tosses the piece out of the window.

During Father Alfonzo Agosti's first appointment, Faustina slithered onto her balcony and sashayed into my life with an orange towel wrapped around her head, wearing only a man's oversized shirt with the sleeves rolled up high, making great puffs that encircled her slender arms. She made a great event of hanging out her laundry. And with the slip hanging from the cord, she backed into her apartment and smiled at her imaginary audience, bowing her head in appreciation. I quickly lowered my head below the window ledge.

Sunday

No one comes on a Sunday. The solitude embraces me like my pilling blue blanket. My thoughts are foggy and I could happily watch paint dry.

I force open my eyes to the yellow glare in the room.

It's sparse.

My room is spartan but certainly not devoid of personal objects. My walls are covered in prints. The 1966 Pirelli Calendar is on the table, opened to May. A great bookshelf takes up most of one wall and is crammed with books I intend to read and lives I intend to pry open.

I lie on the bed and rest my head on the window ledge. The last piece of fruit, a fig, is wrinkly and dark and split in two places.

Faustina's walls have always seemed vacant and lonely, covered with blue, peeling wallpaper. A poster of a matador and the map of the world are pinned to the walls. An aged brown teddy bear sits upright on the sofa. A blue vase is filled with silk sunflowers.

But today her room is deserted. More vacant than usual.

The doors of Faustina's balcony lie open unevenly as though they are partially unhinged. Her apartment door is ajar.

I get out of bed and put on a robe. The air in the room is icy so I light the oven. As the water boils for my tea, I stare out of the kitchen window but she is nowhere to be seen. There is nothing in her room. Not even a whisper.

My chest pounds restlessly and I draw a breath that encircles my lungs like the first drag of a cigarette. The posters are gone, leaving pale rectangular ghosts on the walls. The furnishings are gone, along with the bear and the flowers. The room is a gaping chasm.

The kettle whistles, more and more urgent, but I don't feel much like a tea any more.

I am alone. More alone that I would like, even for a Sunday.

Pink Oleander

Here's the thing, see, I never thought that I'd be one of them, the ones that I always sniggered about. The ones with the gelatinous bellies cascading over their blue nylon trackie dacks. The ones that wait down at the Plaza. They sip cheap, overheated cappuccinos out of white cups, drink them slowly because the day is long and the conversation's unhurried. An appalling mass of unfussy grey hair sits atop Botox-free foreheads.

I try to eavesdrop but don't always hear what they're whispering. But they gesticulate significantly. Along with their presence, nothing they say is useful. And I know this because I'm like them. I skipped straight from coveting a convertible to buying leisurewear from Best and Less. No affairs, no finding myself dancing cheek to cheek with the one I love. With nobody to watch over me, I stumbled through the doors from the car park dotted with dense pink oleander and knew that I was home. The brow that I practiced so hard not to crease for fear of creating permanent lines relaxed immediately and furrowed all on its own. I sighed with relief at the letting go. Nobody should have to walk around unfurrowed for so long. It was like taking off a girdle. Just like that.

Mondays are busy here—the fruit shop opens early after its Sunday closure. They're Catholic, you see, and John likes to go to the Parish Church with the family. I remember seeing them there on the odd occasion that I made the pilgrimage. All dressed up like *The Sullivans* in their Sunday best and all that. Spit and polish. He wore a suit, John did; the slacks were creased

9

deliberately and flawlessly. She would often wear that navy-blue pleated skirt that made her thighs expand as she sat and knelt, but it skimmed her just so when she collected Communion. The kids didn't make a move without consulting Him with their eyes. Plaintive eyes that shouted, "I'd rather be mowing than doing this." But they quickly rubbed it away when He looked at them. I knew that look. That fear when you've said too much, stripping away the whitewash uncovering angry black graffiti and the look lashes and burns your skin—the look that says, "Wait until we get home." That was the look they had and my heart bled tears that flooded my throat so much that I had to leave. No benediction. No Communion. No Confession. I smoked outside with the others.

They stayed and talked to the other parishioners after Mass. The kids screamed in the hall, pounding their feet against the unpolished floorboards on the stage, making deep rumbles in its bowels. I lingered close to Father Matthew, whose creamy cassock needed to be hemmed at the back. I could do that for him. I brushed my hand quickly against his back.

"Sorry."

I walked towards the hall just as John pushed his hand into the priest's. The slightest glimmer of green plastic stuck out from between their hands. I took a deep breath and kept walking, walked through the steel school gates, recognising the grey beards, the nylon shirts, the fake Gucci bags and yellow filigreed gold dripping off necks and fingers and ears. I walked along Churchill Avenue; front yards littered with broken Fisher Price toys and stained mattresses. Hard rubbish permitted here at all times, read the sign in the rubbish bin bay of the flats. Wasn't that always the way here? I lived amongst the city's hard rubbish. The West is chock-full of hard rubbish.

I snooped through the debris, artefacts that exposed transient lives were strewn next to a carton half full of rotten clingstone peaches and a pair of slippers with tattered rubber soles. Transient lives. Except for the homeless man whose ramshackle living room is in the grassland next to Tottenham Station. Can a homeless man live in the one place for years?

People in the West are on the move. On the move to bigger and cheaper double-brick houses in Werribee or Point Cook. And when fortune strikes, we're on the move to Yarraville or Seddon, wanting to live the dream. But lately, we're staying put in convenient houses with double garages, no yard, and steel shutters that stay down all day and night. The West is staying put.

But there's always the dream of upscaling. The dream's made even more real with every tattered garage sale sign taped to light posts.

The West is dotted with pink oleander glowing fiercely against a sky pockmarked by grey clouds and the Olex tower. The smells of pork roll pate, coriander and lime wafts up my nostrils on the odd day that the wind is blowing the delights of the Brooklyn tip in another direction. And there's always melodrama. If it's not friends stabbing each other on Rupert Street across from the homeless guy's home, it's some poor bastard Indian student being bashed in St Albans, or the clang of freight trains in the dead of night, and traffic lights clocking sleepless seconds.

I wait at night, alone with the curtains drawn against the streetlight that's right outside my bedroom window. They don't fix much around here but they fix that light quickly when it breaks accidentally.

It was quiet at the Plaza and the fruit shop was closed for two weeks after John's son fell from the huge tree on their nature strip. You don't see kids playing outside any more, let alone in trees, and definitely not without adult supervision. We could all see why. It was such a tragedy. That's what they all said. She should have been there, looking after him, not the cash register. The tragic news made the front page of the *Leader* and the *Mail*. But we found out beforehand.

Tragedy strikes popular local fruiterer.

It was a tragedy. And I just wanted to say something reassuring to him about grief and loss and loneliness. I waited for him after Mass week after week, but I didn't see him, not even when the shop reopened. His wife slumped on a stool at the register, dressed in black from head to toe, and her face was free of makeup. She rang through items without looking and no longer counted back the change. He stopped carrying watermelons on his thick shoulders and wheeled them in with a trolley instead. His hair turned white and translucent, stripped of all pigment where once it was black and proud. He passed his wife and looked down at his feet. He blamed her too.

He stopped talking to his audience out front. He stopped enchanting us. He stopped slapping shoulders and rubbing perfectly combed *Brylcreemed* hair. He buried himself with the deliveries out the back and came out only when he was short-staffed or had a particularly heavy stock delivery.

Slowly he disappeared until finally even his wife became a notable absence. *What was her name?* Despite her winter motif jumpers in reds and blues she never managed to crack a smile, no cheer. And I couldn't fathom exactly how long she had been gone. One day, I just noticed that a black-haired fifteen-year-old in a baby-doll top and leggings was fumbling around the keys of the cash register. Just some random girl popping gum and listening to her iPod to avoid the pension-day chitchat.

It didn't make a difference to us, though. Not really. The deli still served its spanakopitas and heavily diluted coffee and the chicken shop kept roasting chooks. If it wasn't for the sign that read "Under New Management", it was as though they had never been there.

The pink oleander seems to bloom for most of the year, its cheeriness belying the frosty morning air. I ate on the run from an opaque, camel-coloured Tupperware container that I'd found at the St Vinnies for a dollar. You couldn't microwave this one but I was only eating cantaloupe. Sweet and ripe and nothing like the ones John used to sell at the fruit shop. Not the Glad-wrapped ones on the "reduced" table that had random chunks missing. Half price for half a cantaloupe. It did seem like such a bargain, or maybe I was prepared to buy anything because I was just so grateful to see him. To see the way he barely looked at her. The way he whispered about her while he sampled nuts. Pistachios were his favourite. Me too.

But I can't say that we missed him, me and the detritus who carefully sipped our burnt cappuccinos. Me with my cracked Birkenstocks and them with cascading bellies. We just went on as before and I became ingrained like the pick a prize machine.

One Sunday, long after they'd been forgotten, I waited outside their house and followed them down to the creek up at Matthews Hill, over where the storm water drain passes under Sunshine Road. Even where I was, behind the willow, I could feel the glow of the bonfire and ash that fell on my cheeks. They inflamed the fire with the contents of bottles that they then smashed against the rocks of the dry creek bed. Their cheering swelled as the alcohol encouraged the flames, which obscured the white-blue clouds.

I ran through a bonfire once, on a dare.

I covered my head with the hood of my windcheater and just ran through. It was at school camp and none of them thought I would do it. They laughed as Mary Pritchard told them how I cried when Sister Paul had tried to force me to eat baked beans and spaghetti from a can that morning. She made me stare at the plate of mushed food all through breakfast and shoved a piece of buttered toast into my hand only when the meal came to an end with a clang and it was clear that I would not budge. She would tell my mother, she said. Try telling her I rejected tinned spaghetti and see where that gets you, Sister Lesbian.

"I bet I can run through the bonfire," I called out, my shrill voice rising above Mary Pritchard's, and everyone turned in my direction, clearly forgetting all about the tinned baked beans and spaghetti, which was a good thing because when I thought of them I just wanted to spew.

"Yeah, right," said Lorna Mifsud. "How are you gonna do that? Go into some sort of trance? Get someone to wave a watch in front of your face and make you cluck like a chicken first."

I shrugged and tried not to think of the logistics. Don't think about how, just do it and do it properly or they'll be smashing you into lockers for the rest of the term. What was the worst thing that could happen? I could fall face first into the fire and they'd think I was an idiot—nothing changed—or I could jump through the fire and come out relatively unscathed and I'd be the talk of the school for years. "Oh my God, did you hear about Josie Candiano? She ran through a bonfire at camp." "Josie Candiano? Did she get caught?" And they'd talk about how I did it while Miss Dunn watched the whole thing, glued to the spot.

It's serene down at the creek. Even with the kids shouting at each other across the blazing fire, I could hear the cicadas chirruping in the thick grass. I leaned against the trunk of the willow and let my head fall forward wearily.

When had I started to follow them? When I first saw Paul coming out of the underground parking with a sprig of jasmine tucked into the back pocket of his slacks. At first it was down to his car. A silver-blue Mercedes; old, with squealing brakes and a cracked back window. Then it was the whole way home, a square box in Braybrook facing South Road. I watched her kiss him at the door but he barely stopped as she stretched herself onto her tiptoes. I couldn't hear what they said, of course; I was a reasonable distance away. But there was a silent grunt of acknowledgement.

I'm them now. I come here and sit. I complain about how nothing's the same any more—the Indians with their iPhones like shimmery veins of ore; the Tongans with their menacing physiques; and the Sudanese girls with their runway bodies in super-tight Lolitta fashions. Remember how there were just dagos and skips? The skips would terrorise us with switchblades just for the hell of it, no iPhones, no fussy runners. They did it just for the hell of it. They waited for dad once, long before I was born. It was after the Liberace show in the city. They chased him onto the 19 tram.

It's serene. Through the rectangular skylight, the sunlight casts a protective glow over the tables and dust mites fly freely over a rainbow of polyester. The complaints sound like sighs exchanged between lovers who don't shy from warm morning breath.

We don't mention the fruiterer or his wife. Now and then someone will bring up the tragedy but the conversation soon wanes and we talk once more about the streets, how the oleander drops its pink petals on the sidewalk in front of our houses. Street after street of lolly-pink debris. The council should just come and chop 'em all down. Messy plants, plugging up the drains.

A Death in the
Trabacche Caves

They found her on the floor of the Trabacche caves during the moon landing. That there was a blackout at the precise moment of man's first step on the uneven crater was no coincidence. Café Garibaldi heaved with men who smelled of horses and DDT and children poked their heads around calloused elbows. The sharp aroma of black coffee and fried sweets hung in the still air. An austere voice slowly translated the foreign words that echoed from the black-and-white screen. The coffee machine hissed and spat furiously, mimicking the collective gasp of the crowd when the television screen turned black.

"Oh you're kidding."

"It's those bloody fascists!" someone cried.

"It's a conspiracy!"

"Or Don Ciccio's crowd."

"*Tziddo*. Someone might hear."

"Tse."

A couple of the younger boys peered around the back of the television, scratching their heads and murmuring to one another and pointing when a girl in a green dress ran through the piazza and yelled, "There's been a death in the Trabacche caves. Doctor Santangelo, come quick."

*****

If it were not for the moon landing, the day the girl died in the Trabacche caves would have been like any other day in Mosolina. The sun crept slowly across a sulphuric sky dotted with playful clouds. It was summer's day like so many others before it. The weekends were long and becoming more and more tedious. It seemed they would never end and the girls were trapped with the walls of the palazzo, the garden of lonely vestal virgins with its crumbling stone walls and jasmine grappling with wrought iron. The naked statues only added to their discomfort.

The damp dress caressed Giulia's thigh as she waded into the middle of the fountain. Josie's mashed face was simple, framed by thin and wilting strands of hair with a loose purple headband around her skull. The corners of her eyes came down to meet hollow cheeks, eternally sad. Her t-shirt was soaked all the way to her ribs and she clutched Triton's stiff leg while water rained from the conch under the statue's arm.

What a waste, Giulia thought while she pulled her without success. She could have been pretty but she just looked as dumb as the church sweeper, pushing his dirty broom around at night. Dragging trails of ancient cobwebs and dirt.

"Why don't you just leave her alone," Maria called from the towel beside the fountain where she lay on her stomach kicking her legs in the air to the quick tempo of the music. "It's pointless."

"It's not my fault," Josie wailed. "It's not my fault."

"Come on," Giulia yelled above the music. "If you don't come we can't go."

"It's not my fault."

"Well whose fucking fault is it, then?" Giulia whispered.

"Forget it. I don't want to go anyway," said Maria. "What's this song called?"

"Josie!" Giulia lost her patience and let go. "You're just going to ruin it for everyone."

"Giulia!"

"What?" Giulia turned to Maria, who continued to rewind the tape while it was still playing, and it screeched like the devil.

"Forget about it. What's the name of this song?" Maria asked with her pen poised for a response.

"Oh, I don't know," said Giulia.

Josie crawled out of the fountain and ran to house beneath the eaves that dripped with shiny purple grapes. "It's not my fault," she yelled.

"What IS she talking about?" Giulia just wanted a normal day this summer. Just one normal day.

"Don't worry about her," Maria said. "What's the name of this song?"

Giulia closed her eyes and counted backwards slowly like Sister Graziella had told her. She concentrated on the weaving melody and strange words, deep and conspiratorial as her father's after grappa and cigarettes.

"I don't know," Giulia lied. "When are we leaving?" Still her eyes were closed.

The grounds chimed with the songs of the fluttering pernices and zigoli. Zebra butterflies brushed Giulia's hair and silken-tailed fish zipped around the fountain in figure eights. Bullet wounds covered the stone building; chunks of the parapet were nowhere to be seen. Brushed away years before.

Maria placed her hand on Giulia's arm. "If my dad finds out, he'll kill me."

"You're dead here anyway," Giulia sighed.

Maria slapped her shoulder. Hard. "That's not fair."

Giulia rolled her eyes and mouthed the lyrics silently.

"God," Maria yelled, and threw the pen at the fountain. "I hate you!" she spat towards Josie.

The girl covered her ears. "It's not my fault," she cried.

At the edge of the village, the River Garibaldi flowed beneath the ancient mule road to Gela, where the black marketeers had once hidden during intermittent raids. The road had been bombed by Americans eager to chase the Partisans from the hills and lay in ruins still, having been replaced by a rope bridge soon after its destruction. The cemetery covered the hill to the east, overshadowed by the viaduct.

Five men in tight black suits were walking towards the village.

"Hey," Josie called out, "where are you going?"

"To see the man on the moon," said the man at the back without breaking his stride or raising his head.

The girls continued over the pockmarked landscape and over the boulders above the Trabacche caves to the gypsy quarter.

Josie ran towards the stone outcrops that led deep into the ground. Maria ran after her.

"What are you doing, you idiot? Come here."

"What's down there?" Josie crouched and peered into an opening in the ground.

"Nothing." Giulia rubbed her sunburnt shoulders. "Just catacombs."

"Dead people?" Josie lowered her head into the opening.

"Maybe."

"Mamma?" Josie thrust her head into the dark hole.

Maria pulled her sister by her waist and they continued towards the row of caravans.

An old redheaded woman fluttered a skirt from the small window of her wagon. "Come inside." She waved the skirt at them as though they were supposed to use it to climb in.

"Josie, you need to stay outside," said Maria.

Josie flopped down on a step and wrapped her arms around her legs. Giulia stared at her, overcome by a powerful desire to cradle her in her arms.

The cramped wagon was as ripe as a fig. A shelf housed a brushed copper pot with a long handle, and three ceramic cups, not much bigger than thimbles; a porcelain doll with dusty white skin and black hair, holding a crumbling posy of miniature rose buds; a mother-of-pearl frame with a black-and-white photograph of a young family—a man with dark, hollow eyes, wearing a tight suit, and a woman with long, dark hair and a formless black dress, holding an infant wrapped in an enormous swathe. A straw broom rested against the doorway and a doctor's satchel lay open, spilling over with tattered-looking clothing.

"Do you like to collect things?" the witch asked.

"I collect frog things," said Maria.

"Ah. You should place a frog at your doorstep. It will attract wealth. Make sure it faces inwards or the fortune will fly from your home. It's a common mistake. What about you?"

"No, not really," Giulia said distractedly.

"Not terribly nostalgic, are you?" The gypsy leaned against a shelf and its contents shuddered. "That's good. If your spirit dwells in the past, often you find yourself bound by it and your soul is restless in the present."

"You seem to cling to the past." Giulia turned to the cluttered walls.

"No, treasure. I sprinkle cinnamon, curry powder and oregano for a quick and peaceful separation, sage for an emotional bond that does not break easily. And I carry an amulet." She patted her chest. "It shields me both from the past and the present, like those lovely veils you wear in church. Now sit, both of you." She pointed towards two folded chairs that hung from hooks on the wall.

"Anyway, my name is Liliana." Her teeth gleamed when she opened her mouth.

"My name's Maria—"

Liliana raised her hand. "I don't need to know. Now, lean closer, you two. You see that statue?" The gypsy waved her fingers to a small black figurine of the Madonna, and the girls nodded. "Well, don't touch it. In fact, try not to touch anything unless I ask you or I won't be responsible for what might happen."

"See," Maria muttered, "what if something happens? How will we explain it to your mother?"

"For God's sake. What could happen?" whispered Giulia.

"Stop whispering," said Liliana. "I can hear everything." She pulled her ears forward. "Superhuman, ever since I tried a Hellebore flying ointment. I can't fly but I have the spectacular hearing of a vampire."

The gypsy's hair frothed around narrow shoulders all the way to her waist. Her eyes were as green as a cat's, and the smudged black kohl looked like it hadn't been removed in years. Rich embroidered Crewelwork in fine, worsted yarn stood out vividly on her jacket, reminding Giulia of the vivid paintings on the walls of Santa Lucia.

"We really can't stay too long," said Giulia. "My mother doesn't know where I am."

"Of course not. If anyone asks, just say you were at confession." Liliana shook her head while she laughed. "Young girls haven't changed at all since I was one."

The gypsy sat facing them on the bed at the far end of the room. She tucked an overstuffed cushion behind her back and eased into it with a sigh. She lifted a deck of cards from a box on the bed.

Giulia sat stiffly in a folding chair. Her eyes had finally become accustomed to the filtered light that shimmered off the small glass windows and struck at the objects within.

Liliana placed two porcelain cups in front of them and poured from a silver teapot. Dark green leaves floated to the bottom of the cups and the girls looked at one another.

"Now," said Liliana, "drink that and leave a few drops.

"Turn the cup three times, like this." She swished her own cup around.

"Now turn your cups upside down onto the saucers."

The remaining drops drained into the saucer and they waited.

Giulia strained to follow her words; her accent didn't belong to the village, or any other nearby village. She heard muffled voices outside while Liliana shuffled the cards. After a long silence, Liliana examined the inside of the cup, turning it carefully in different directions.

Giulia folded her hands at her lap, trying to hide her impatience at the old crone's theatre. She sensed a gentle quivering against her thigh at the *tap-tap-tap-tap-tap* of Maria's foot against the table leg.

Liliana turned the cup repeatedly, making exaggerated sighs and creasing her face in a frown.

"Mischief is brewing," said Liliana.

Giulia looked up and laughed.

"Do you think it's funny?"

"No. No." Giulia waved away her smile. "I mean, it just sounds so silly."

Maria stomped on her foot.

"Ow! What?"

"You made me come. So just take it seriously and let me enjoy it," Maria pleaded.

"Well, it's dumb. I mean, why is it that there's always something sinister that's about to happen, or that in your past life, you were a queen or something." Giulia pushed her seat back and stood gently, for fear of disturbing any of the ornaments that surrounded them. She lifted the cup and saw only the grit and leaves of her brew.

A scream broke the silence. The gypsy stumbled past them and out the door of the wagon. The girls followed.

A man ran with a sodden, small-framed girl, her head and legs swaying lifelessly. A length of fraying rope hung from her neck and trailed behind them.

Giulia grasped Maria's hand as she moved through the crowd. She shook it away angrily as she fell beside the body. She looked back at Giulia, wide-eyed, her jaw clenched.

"I told you we shouldn't have come here," she hissed.

Giulia fell beside Maria and reached across the lifeless body, slowly releasing the coarse rope that rubbed against thin, bruised skin.

Padre Nostro

I hid them for a whole day. And a night. It was the only time I'd dared.
But we'd been at it so long, threading the uneven silver beads through our
fingers until we were numb and my hands were stiff. *Padre nostro che sei
nei cieli*. Mamma would make me sound it quietly in English, so that I could
be more like the other girls—Our Father who art in Heaven—but I didn't
have the heart to tell her that the other girls were watching *The Sullivans*, not
reciting the rosary night after night with their mothers. And I didn't tell her
that the other girls didn't have votive candles at their bedsides with the face of
Jesus delicately painted on the glass. Maybe they had a picture of Greg Brady
or the Bay City Rollers. But I didn't dare tell her that.

*****

We had come back on the day that Elvis died. Papa was at the airport with
the orange Falcon with the black racing stripes. His hair, dark like fermented
wine, was flat and the curl that normally sat boldly on his forehead, like Dean
Martin's, was limp and uncombed as though he'd forgotten the Brylcreem.
The skin around his eyes was the colour of pomegranates and puffed below
his dewy eyelashes. He'd just heard, he said. Mamma rested her head on his
neck and they touched each other like it had been months, which it had. And
I sat on top of the luggage, dipping my fingers into the packet of Wizz Fizz
that had become lumpy with moisture.

I wasn't sure if they wept because of Elvis or because of Nonna. Papa called us while we were still in Italy, just days before Nonna died, called to tell Mamma he was sorry and that he wished he could be there but the farm couldn't manage itself—he didn't trust any of the Turks to look after it. I could just see him there in that rusty tin house in the middle of nowhere. It rattled against the wind that could probably rip off its corrugated roof. I imagined him with the TV tray, the one with the paddle steamer and the old-time travellers looking so festive. He'd be sitting in front of the dusty fireplace eating a bowl of spaghetti and watching the news, hopeful that something would filter through about the Mother Country. Anything. Sometimes, I would watch him from the doorway when he thought he was alone and see oil trailing down his chin but he'd be too tired to notice, too lonely to care.

On the other side of the world, Mamma slowly peeked into an old trunk. She lifted the thick damask and inhaled deeply. What is it, Mamma? I asked. Lemons, she replied. To me, it just smelled damp. The rain pelted our heads as we bolted onto the train on our way to catch the plane back home, back to Papa. Mamma held her head and arms over the window and waved at her sister, like she knew it would be the last time. They locked their fingers together until the train moved with a jerk off the platform. The tears rolled onto Mamma's satin shirt. You can never get tears out of satin. Or was it silk? So many lessons.

She didn't have the energy to warm the kitchen on those first few days we were back. She stayed in bed in the room that faced the empty paddock and would cry out occasionally, oh Mamma, as though the words were like oxygen for the dead.

I couldn't endure her pleas, so I left her with a glass of water and some Aspro and took the dogs for a run, stopping by the Turks' house and motioning through the door to the boy, careful that nobody should see me.

In the channel, the yabbies were jumping with joy into our dirty black buckets as the yellow nylon rope cut into our hands when we pulled against the current. The wind wound its way through the loquat tree and it seemed to talk, only it spoke words that only Mamma could understand—go put a jacket on, the rain's coming. But I never heard the words because it didn't speak to me.

After the boy went home, I sat on the edge of the murky channel where the river snakes slipped through, making S's with their rubbery bodies, and the cows mooed me into a restful sleep that lately seemed to evade me at night—the sounds that came from the dark wardrobe would drive me into an inescapable insomnia that would find me running for the school bus in the morning, hoping that I could keep my breakfast down, the taste of Vegemite thick on my tongue.

*****

I took them after the third month. By this time I'd committed each of the Mysteries to memory and my skin had been scorched by the embers that jumped from the fireplace each night – exploding redbacks, Mamma said. We would press each of the beads as we repeated prayer after prayer, watching the sun disappear after another day. They were the silver ones; the ones that she had brought with her and that she kept in a small square jewellery box with the name of the jeweller embossed in gold on the lid.

It was the sort of cloudy day in November when the sun gropes you with fingers so leaden that it leaves the inevitable red ring at the edges of your sleeves and a flush on your cheeks. I hid down the side paddock, the one next to the haystack and with grass so tall and green and filled with sweet dew. I knew that nobody would ever find me. I left a trail as wide as my outstretched arms, flattening the thin blades with my weight as I crawled through.

I peeked over the grass at old Mario Lentini, who sat in the gutted-out Torana with a transistor on the dashboard. His legs hung through the shattered windscreen, and he was tapping them with a heavy hand. He sung high into the sky, and from the side he looked like he was howling. Fancied himself a bit of a rocker, with a curl that hung low over his brow, black and shiny like a rooster's comb. They say he sounded like Frank Sinatra, but to me he sounded like he was singing in slow motion.

I lay on my back and made animals out of the clouds. I counted the number of beads on the rosary but lost track. Smaller than the ones I had hanging from my bedpost. I had big plans—one day soon, maybe when I was thirteen, I would pull them off the bedpost and replace them with a stuffed toy. Humphrey or Fat Cat. The rosary beads hung close to my head at night, each bead the size of a dry chickpea, heavy with repentance. I ran my fingers over them and they were uneven, all coarse edges, marking my palms. Like scars.

I chewed on a lemon flower and wondered if a dog had peed on it, like Mamma always warned, but it tasted good anyway. Despite the heavy rains early in winter that Papa had often told us about when he'd rung, much of the earth was already scorched. Nothing like home, Mamma would remind me.

This place was all still so new to them and they were still indelibly connected to things I'd never even heard of—almond milk, yellow brioche dipped in tart but saccharine-sweet granita for breakfast and school notebooks with little grids instead of lines.

Papa told me stories about walking the streets in summer without sunglasses because the sun was not so cruel, his eyes would be wide open and the air would smell like open fires and fresh milk—not the sort of fresh milk that came in a bottle, but straight from a sleepy cow and into a grey pail.

I wrapped the rosary around my fist and punched the air like a boxer, pressing the crucifix in my palm. Our Father who art in Heaven… Each of the Mysteries of the rosary imprinted just like the seven times table. Seven times seven is forty-nine. Sister Margaret was fond of slapping the times tables into us wog girls—slapped the back of our calves with the wooden ruler until they glowed like sunburn. I still remember the seven times table. And I can still remember the prayers of the rosary. I can still remember redemption but I don't believe so much any more—like all good Catholic girls.

I climbed over the fence, where the cow had been gutted recently and the flies hummed melodies with the cicadas. Trails of intestines lay delicately over the stones like Mamma's stockings on the Hill's Hoist. I sniffed the air and drew the stench of death deep in my lungs, heavy and fearful like the dog when Papa came home late at night.

I opened the gate quietly, worried that the rickety, rusted hinges would sound out their alarm to Mamma and I would be found out. She was still filled with guilt that she had been so distant when her mother fell ill, but she had enough vigour left to pursue me with the splintered spoon she kept near the laundry door ready to punish untold transgressions. I latched the gate carefully and ran quickly to the chicken coop, watchful for the slithering gold bands of the tiger snake. I held the beads close in the pocket of my ruffled skirt, which caught against the dry scrub. My socks were thick with burrs that scratched my skin. But there was no time to stop to pick them off.

Shadows in the chicken coop. The red hen fluffed its feathers at me as I wandered through the gate. Filomena. Mamma had named her after the nun who used to teach her to embroider the thick sheets that were itchy against my legs at night. Filomena, qua-qua, she would call out, and the hen would immediately vacate her nest to display a small pile of creamy eggs, clean as though she had polished them.

But today, Filomena didn't move from her perch. It was the wrong time of the day for that. I watched her closely, fearful of her sharp beak as I approached the back corner of the coop. Cool against my fingers, I tucked the beads next to the crumpled packed of Benson & Hedges and a near-empty box of matches in the hold and replaced the wooden shingle and covered it with straw for good measure.

I ran back to the house as though I was running quickly over summer bitumen. Mamma was in the windowless kitchen pushing a piece of wood into the stove. The room smelled of yeast, and smoke came from the oven. Bread. My eyes burned from the roasted chillies that clung to the dampness. When she turned to me, her eyes were swollen. She wiped her arm across her nose and fished a jewellery box from her apron and opened it. A wad of cotton wool sat in the plastic box but it was empty. Mamma held out her hands, like she did when she wanted me to know that she was telling the truth. Gone, she mouthed, gone. It must have been that boy.

She pointed at the Turks' house. She put the box back into her pocket and turned away to watch the burning wood.

Heaviness. Like the solar eclipse on my Communion day when we took cover beneath the fig tree for fear that the sky was falling. The weight of my mother's loss enclosed me and hummed slowly the tunes with words I no longer recognised.

Sinless. And me, at eight, I wrapped her in my arms and allowed her to press her fingers deeply into my flesh, making purple marks. And I felt warm droplets on my neck, which washed it all away.

There is a fog where my brain used to be— An Ode to Chemistry (and baking)

There is a fog where my brain used to be,

A cupcake right beside the gaping crevice of

a hypothalamus that was vacated

the day red velvet came to stay.

There is port wine jelly

that wiggles and jiggles but holds together the space where my Corpus Callosum once was; Sweet and crisp

on my palate

like barely cooked apples in a pie at a roadhouse on the way to Wernicke's Area.

But I digress.

Mainly because the paretial lobe took away my sex;

an iceberg stole my paretial lobe

and froze my ovaries

after I stuck the carving knife in

the roaster.

Four pieces of cheesecake, lemon and ricotta—the fancy sort, not regular lobes.

Cheesecake as creamy as sweetbreads,
flecked with candied lemon rind and
sprinkled with hundreds & thousands.

They stuck an icepick in
my temporal lobe
and I heard the sound of silence;

suspended there;

in time and space.

They took the smallest piece, but I stuffed it with sugar and spice and twenty-one-dollar bottles of liquor from the local.

Death comes
(*with instructions*)

**(While listening to: Sigur Rós, Album – Hlemmur soundtrack,
Tracks – Hannes and Óskabörn þjóðarinnar)**

Death comes, at times,
>When the Elysian Fields have made room,
>With a rug and basket full
>Of all the wonders you once loved,
>Loved more than life itself,
>When life seemed so drawn and careless.
>And crowded.
>You stuttered, then, like it hardly mattered—
>Stuttered in the driveway only to cover yourself.
>Then, buried deep beneath the galleon ship,
>Bloated bodies on the surface,
>Float
>Past your pop tart life.
>You count them like days
>Since,
>Since memory's beginning,
>Where the only cat to tinkle the ivory,
>The only cat to walk on your grave,

The last cat came to say

And sing

Of rainbow connections

Of Higher Floors

Of purple haze and

Purple rain dripping over

Keys of ivory.

Death comes with woven baskets filled with white lilies and yellow daisies and sprays of baby's breath,

With a waterproof casket of gold

And feather pillows.

Death comes

At times

With thousands of revelations under a shroud of glass.

Under the Loquat Tree

I woke up and rubbed my eyes with the tips of my pinkies, nails clipped sharp at the edges. Mamma was humming shrilly outside. But she did sound sweet and sincere. She was hanging out the laundry near the puddle of chicken guts that she'd left for the cats. Each high-pitched note castigated me for sleeping in. The sun was swept behind a thin veil of indigo that raced towards the house. I was Dorothy on that fateful day in Kansas. The branches of the fig tree swayed vigorously and I wondered if the wind might rip its ancient roots from the ground.

I would never forget the taste in my mouth, like I'd pressed my tongue against the front steel railing the way I did at the first sign of wintry ice to see if my tongue would stick. Like sucking on a five-cent coin; it left my teeth frigid.

Mamma had made me sleep with three towels over the pillow because she'd never get the blood out. My lips were stuck together, as though I'd sneaked a spoon of peanut butter, and were covered by a thick, crusty layer. Except they were numb. It made me want to laugh out loud, you know. And the thought was far away; it too was overcome by indigo. Except for the pain and the rest of it. But I was used to it by then. You did, you know. You got used to it.

I tiptoed over the lino in pyjamas that were one size too big, dragged under my feet, cushioning my heels that were swollen with welts. The water spluttered from the tap after a lengthy ha-a-a-mmer of the pipes. Shut the bloody taps, Papà would have yelled from the shed over the crack of the axe on redwood, you'll break the fucking pipes. And it would be all bursting copper and water gushing through the walls like it was blood in *The Amityville Horror*. I'll give you a mustacciuni if you're not careful, he'd say. Mustacciuni, he'd say in that half-remembered dialect that nobody seemed to understand any more, emphasising each vowel. But the word had no meaning to me any more, not literally, not like back-hander or knuckle sandwich, or anything like that. We all knew what it meant, though, especially when he spat it out and he'd have saliva covering his purpled chin. That's what he'd have said. But he didn't hear the pipes.

I turned the hot water tap slowly. I pressed a wet hand to my mouth and released it. The sink slowly filled with light-red-turning-dark-red-to-orange. Turner's *Burning of the Houses of Parliament*.

I began to feel my lips, and wished I couldn't—all smooth and swollen like mosquito-bitten veins on the backs of your hands, they swell up more than a normal bite. I have a narrow mouth, not like Farrah Fawcett-Majors', which went from ear to ear. But Jimmy didn't mind. They were like a plump strawberry, he'd say. Always ready for a kiss.

They always were, for the most part, especially when he'd corner me behind the smoking shed next to the presbytery. He had this way of leaning me up against the doorway, out of sight of the other kids so they couldn't dob. We were hidden by the loquat tree, I always thought. But sometimes Father George would emerge suddenly, barely rustling the branches as he picked the small orange fruit, and we'd quickly separate.

Lips waiting to be kissed. That's what he always said.

Papà didn't think to rustle the branches of the tree when he came upon us one afternoon. I had my back to the door and my eyes were closed, like I'd read in *Dolly*. Only scrubbers kissed with their eyes wide open. Although once, I opened them and saw that he too had his eyes scrunched tight, and I watched the way the lines bunched up at the corners from the concentration. His skin was so clear, and smooth like the inside of my thighs, while everyone else was bursting with pubescent sap. He was sixteen but still liked to suck on Sunny Boys—his lips were eternally sticky from orange cordial and were smudged as though from a stolen kiss.

That summer everyone was listening to that song, "Alone With You". It wasn't for us, the adults would say. But we knew what it meant. As though we wouldn't. Jimmy'd watch me swing from the ornamental grapevine that wove its way over Mrs Patterson's back fence and onto the old neglected monkey bars by the bus stop. I'd swing like Tarzan, my loincloth flicked over my belly as I hung with my hands touching the ground. And he'd whistle gently *I'm alone with you to-niiight, I'm alone with you to-niiight, I'm alone with you…* The light gleamed off his earlobe, shattering the air with a million rays.

Papà would have killed me if he knew I was kissing a boy with an earring.

I held on to my hair as Papà pulled me away, fearful that I'd lose too much this time. I wore a scarf last time, and nobody bothered to tear it off. They all knew. But he carried me to bed afterwards, Papà did, he carried me tenderly, worried that he might have broken something. He'd only ever broken a rib once before, that time when I told Miss Kent in home ec class that she was a bitch and I got suspended and he had to leave the factory early to pick me up. You knew he felt bad, though. He'd kneaded my arms like they were mince meat that he'd seasoned with fennel and hot red pepper and salt just before stuffing it into the long, white strands of intestines. He'd sit at my feet and watch my face, mindful of any change. His would crumple; that shadow between terror and pain that I wanted to grasp with all ten fingers until regret wept from each pore. Sometimes I thought he felt no pity, no shame in watching me cower on the ground screaming with my ribs cracked.

After he found me and Jimmy that summer, I couldn't leave the house except for school, and he made me go to the factory straight after and sit in the tea room with the sweaty, blackened men he worked with and watch them smoke silently, watching the clock and lighting another smoke with the last one.

He locked the bedroom door at seven on Friday nights with a bolt that sounded clearly across the pale, icy blue walls of my bedroom. On weekends, I surveyed the day through time-lapse, staring out the window until the sun was ejected from the sky and it was too dark to see anything. But I stared anyway.

The ice cream truck came every day at four, "Greensleeves" jingling from its loudspeaker. We'd run barefoot, dancing on the tacky, hot bitumen. By the end of summer, it didn't matter so much; our soles'd be tough. I'd sit on the fence, like I did, the sunburn on the backs of my thighs stinging from the hot bricks, licking my hands as brown and white streaks rained down the cone and I'd watch the boys from up the street playing cricket, especially Jimmy Munro, whose father drove a hot red panel van with black flames licking the sides. Jimmy wore the tightest white shorts that held everything together so neatly, and when I passed him in the quadrangle at school, he smelled of Old Spice jumbled with boy spice.

I'd have done anything to race after that ice cream truck, but I had to ask just to go to the toilet.

Lizzie was a skip. She'd come over once or twice a week after school and sit in the kitchen while mum sang to Elvis on the radio and made sesame-seed biscuits. They laughed like mother and daughters do. Skip ones. Lizzie had three brothers and two sisters and her mum didn't cook much except charcoal lamb and peas. It was all singing and cooking and the Italian Vita Bella when Lizzie was over.

Even though I didn't move much, I couldn't take a deep breath, on account of my cracked ribs and the lump that kept growing. The medicine they were giving me wasn't helping much. Neither were Father George's mumbled prayers.

After a while, I discovered a way out, a secret passage. I'd seen the cat use it once. Through the wardrobe and into the wall cavity to the spare room. Sometimes I'd sneak out and head down to the park and watch the pink-cheeked girls swing from the monkey bars and wish that my skin was white as milk and that my underwear was covered in little pink flowers like theirs.

But that seemed so distant now. I'd lost all notion of that time when it was simple and reasonable. Instead, I sat at my window with a big drawing pad and I'd draw the houses across the street.

I was good at copying things, Mamma said.

Or I'd steal away in the hours when the earth was coldest and I'd wait for the sun to peek through the city skyline so that I could climb into bed again. The hot-water bottle would chill me by morning.

He said he'd let me out again in the winter, after everything was fixed up.

As winter approached, Mamma's arms would radiate like the kerosene heater and smelled like Avon Unforgettable Beauty Dust. While the fig tree began to lose its foliage, I anxiously helped Mamma with the *Women's Weekly* crossword because she didn't understand the clues—they didn't translate half the time and made no sense. Now and again I'd catch her glimpsing at my shirt, which was stretched tight, but she'd turn away quickly when I caught her.

Sometimes she would even cross herself when I passed her.

There was a scar that ran across the dip right above my top lip, I think from the time my head hit the bed head when I wasn't expecting it—I was never prepared. That's what Papà said.

You walk around with your eyes shut half the time. I should have known better.

Mamma traced the scar with a finger while I sucked on a biro and tried to make sense of the puzzles.

Mamma was inside when Jimmy came over. She was rolling pastry and filling small, round tart shells with smooth, honey-sweet ricotta. A batch of Easter tarts was cooling on the vinyl chair next to the door. I sat at the table opposite her, hoping she would begging her to let me go outside, to the milkbar, to the park, but she responded only with her light brown eyes that seemed often to say nothing—she was only ever thinking about the next meal.

He knocked at the flyscreen, as though it was the most natural thing in the world. His shoulders were hunched over, insolently, like the boys did. He was wearing that AC/DC t-shirt, and he wore it tight, just like Bon Scott; a slight trail tiptoed above his low-slung jeans. And that twinkle on his earlobe—

I heard Papà's Forges slippers sliding over the lino and I had to hold my mouth shut to stop from throwing up. The air in the kitchen turned icy, as though the sun had sucked up all the heat and then disappeared within the folds of a rambling cumulus. My breathing became shallow and echoed in my ears as it did when you held your head under water in the bath, and I could see the air form particles before my face.

A sound came from Mamma's lips. The same sound when she was shooing the Pattersons' cat, which would shit beneath the broccoli just when it was ready to pick.

"Shhhhh!" she called towards the door. But he just went right on ahead and spoke.

"Can I come in?"

A heavy black slipper hit the flyscreen fair and square at eye level. It fell heavily and overturned the tray of tarts, which scattered over the lino.

"You get the hell out of here, boy. Haven't you done enough already."

I didn't have the urge to argue. Maybe it was true. And maybe it was the white cricket shorts, and the dust at the back of his neck, mingling with the cigarettes and the fading aftershave, which I could smell through the fine flywire right now. And maybe it was the way his hand slipped inside my waistband during square dance classes, or the way he brushed his downy cheek down the length of my spine until his head rested in the small of my back. We'd lie that way, in the tall grass, far from anyone, letting the warm summer showers sprinkle featherlike on our skin.

"You've ruined us," Papà said. "Get out of here before I get my rifle."

And then four knuckles seemed to connect with the base of my scull, where it dips at the top of the spine. Then another four knuckles against my left earlobe. I held my belly, held it up with both arms, and balanced myself against the table, grateful for the solid laminate.

I looked up to see the back of Jimmy's t-shirt. It was frayed around the hem and the left raglan sleeve was slightly unstitched at his armpit. He said nothing before he left. He just left me there, in that room that radiated from the stovetop. He left me like a comet's tail that trailed hastily.

Thank you!

Thanks for reading *Girls*. I hope you enjoyed it!

Would you like to know when my next book is available? You can sign up for my new release e-mail list by liking my Facebook page at **http://facebook.com/jovraca-writer**.

Reviews help other readers find books. I appreciate all reviews, whether positive or negative.

This book is lendable through Amazon's lending program. Share it with a friend!

If you want to be kept up to date with my writing, visit my blog: http://jovraca.blogspot.com.au/

When I was a kid (pre-computers), I used to write on the blank end papers of my books. I'd write lists of my favourite TV shows, my best friends, top Abba songs. So use these pages to write your own lists. Feel free.

Printed in Great Britain
by Amazon

39484815R00030